9-13

This book belongs to:

D1487414

For Jessica.
—B.J.S.

immedium

Immedium, Inc.
P.O. Box 31846
San Francisco, CA 94131
www.immedium.com

Justin Time series, text, illustrations © 2012 Guru Animation Studio Ltd. All rights reserved.
Story based on an episode of *Justin Time* written by Erika Strobel.
Justin Time developed by Mary Bredin, Frank Falcone, and Brandon James Scott.
www.justintime.net

First hardcover edition published 2012.

Editor: Don Menn
Designer: Erica Loh Jones

Printed in Malaysia
10 9 8 7 6 5 4 3 2 1

Library of Congress Cataloging-in-Publication Data

Scott, Brandon, 1982-
The pancake express / adapted and illustrated by Brandon James Scott ; [story based on an
episode of Justin Time written by Erika Strobel]. -- 1st hardcover ed.
p. cm. -- (Justin time)
Summary: "Justin imagines that he drives a Canadian steam train and helps his friend Olive
deliver maple syrup to a pancake festival"-- Provided by publisher.
ISBN 978-1-59702-035-0 (hardback)
I. Strobel, Erika. II. Justin time (Television program) III. Title.
PZ7.S41635Pan 2012
[E]--dc23

2012009822

ISBN: 978-1-59702-035-0

THE PANCAKE EXPRESS

ADAPTED AND ILLUSTRATED BY
BRANDON JAMES SCOTT

immedium
San Francisco, CA

"Ready to play, Squidgy?" asks Justin as he sets up his track.

"Want to play with this train?" says Squidgy.

"That train's okay, but we need something…"

"Bigger," says Justin.

"Faster," says Squidgy.

WE NEED a REAL TRAIN!

"Come on, Squidgy," announces Justin. "Let's go for a train ride!"

"Okay," Squidgy agrees. "You be the driver."

Justin shouts, "All aboard!"

They scoot across the floor, gathering steam.

Chugga Chugga Chugga Chugga

CHOO CHOO!

Justin and Squidgy race along in their very
own steam train! They pull a coal car,
a cargo car, and even a caboose!

Justin is the engineer. He drives the train.
Squidgy tugs on the steam whistle.

Justin and Squidgy arrive at the train station. Their best friend Olive is waiting for them on the platform. "Hi Olive!"

She waves at them, and calls across the tracks, "Hi Justin! Hi Squidgy! Welcome to Canada!"

"I run this maple syrup stop on the railway. Our syrup tastes so delicious. We deliver it everywhere."

"Today there is a big Pancake Festival in Flapjack Falls," adds Olive. "And I need to bring them my maple syrup."

"But I'm going to be late!"

"Well, you're in luck Olive!" says Justin. "We're the fastest train on the railroad. We'll help you!"

"And we love maple syrup!" gushes Squidgy. He is so excited that he pops into a big maple leaf!

Olive pours the maple syrup down from her tower and into the barrel on Justin's train. "Okay, the maple syrup's all loaded," says Olive.

"Ready to go?" Justin asks.

"Wait," says Olive. "Before we go, we have to make sure the train is ready too. We need to feed the furnace."

"What do you feed a furnace?" asks Squidgy. "Pancakes?"

"No, Squidgy,"
Olive giggles.
"Coal!"

"The coal lights the fire... the fire heats the water... the water turns to steam... steam pumps the engine, and the engine pumps the wheels!"

They load the furnace with coal, and off they go!

"We're really rolling now!" laughs Justin.

They pass mighty, snow-capped mountains rising high above evergreen forests and cool, blue lakes.

"Look," Olive shouts, pointing up ahead.
"We're almost there."

They all cheer, "Next stop, Flapjack Falls!"

"Stop the train!" yells Olive. Justin pulls on the breaks.

SCREEEEEECH!

There's a fallen tree on the tracks, blocking the way.

"Uh – Oh," groans Squidgy. "How will we get by?"

Suddenly a beaver pops up from behind the log.

"Hey, I have an idea," says Justin.
"Beavers can cut through wood
with their big teeth.
Maybe he can help
us clear the path?"

The beaver happily agrees and starts chomping the log into small pieces of wood.

Olive encourages everyone, "If we hurry and tidy up all this wood, we can still make it to the Pancake Festival."

Luckily, a friendly moose wanders out of the forest and offers to help.

Everyone works together to put the wood onto Justin's train.

"Thanks for your help!" says Olive.

Justin invites the beaver and the moose to come with them to the Pancake Festival. Everybody hops on the train.

Justin cranks the lever and hollers,

ALL ABOARD!

"Uh-oh," shouts Justin.
"The train won't start!"

"Oh no!" says Squidgy,
looking in the coal bucket.
"No coal, means no fire,
means no steam, means...
NO PANCAKES!"

Squidgy panics, and accidently sends a log rolling...

down the pile,

across the coal car,

and into the furnace!

Suddenly a flame lights up!
"Hey look!" exclaims Justin. "Wood burns, too!"

"And we have lots of wood!" adds Olive.

So they load the furnace with wood,
and the train steams ahead.

There is a huge cheer as the train arrives.
Now the Pancake Festival can begin!
Everybody wants some of Olive's famous
maple syrup for their pancakes!

"Thank you so much!" says Olive to Justin and Squidgy. "Without your help our special maple syrup delivery would never have made it!"

Justin answers, "Oh, it was no problem for... the Pancake Express!"

Now Justin and Squidgy are ready to go home.

"Bye Olive," says Justin.

"See you soon!" says Squidgy.

"See you next time," says Olive as she waves goodbye.

Back at home, Justin and Squidgy set their train on the tracks. "All this talk of pancakes is making me hungry!" says Squidgy.

"All aboard the Pancake Express," calls Justin.
"Next stop, the kitchen!"

The end.